KV-670-678

ORCHARD BOOKS
338 Euston Road, London NW1 3BH
Orchard Books Australia
Level 17/207 Kent Street, Sydney, NSW 2000

First published in 2011 by Orchard Books
First published in paperback in 2012

Text and illustrations © Clara Vulliamy 2011

The right of Clara Vulliamy to be identified as the author and
illustrator of this work has been asserted by her in accordance with
the Copyright, Designs and Patents Act, 1988.

A CIP catalogue record for this book is
available from the British Library.

ISBN 978 1 40831 245 2

1 3 5 7 9 10 8 6 4 2

Printed in China

Orchard Books is a division of Hachette Children's Books,
an Hachette UK Company.
www.hachette.co.uk

This is Muffin,
the yummiest small brown bear.

Muffin jumps out of bed
and hurries to the letterbox.

An **INVITATION**
has arrived!

"It's from **Fizz** and **Flora!**" says Muffin.

"A **PRESENT.**
I must take a present for the twins."
Luckily, he has saved a large paper
bag full of sugar buns!

AT LAST, it's time to set off for the party.

On the way, Muffin stops for a rest.
His tummy feels empty.
The sugar buns smell nice.

He will just have a little look.

"I'll just have one bite,"
says Muffin . . .

yum!

"... and another bite ...

Yum!

... and just one more ...."

Yum! Yum! Yum! Yum! Yum! Yum!

By the time
Muffin arrives,

the bag feels flatter.

He puts it with the other presents.

"HAPPY BIRTHDAY, Fizz!" says Muffin.

"HAPPY BIRTHDAY, Flora!"

"First, we will play **GAMES**,"
says Flora.

They play hide and seek . . .

. . . and musical statues,

keeping very still
when the music stops.

Then they have the
PARTY TEA.

"Now we will have PRESENTS," says Flora.

Flora gives Fizz some shiny red ribbon.

Fizz gives Flora a stick.

Muffin fetches his present.

He looks inside the bag.

It's COMPLETELY EMPTY!

He must have eaten ALL

the sugar buns by mistake!

"Twins!
I have a **special surprise**
for you," says Muffin.

"You have a flag pole, and some
shiny red ribbon for tying . . .

. . . and here is
THE FLAG!

"It's stripy, especially for rabbits,
and especially . . .

"This is the best party EVER!"
say Fizz and Flora.
"Thank you, Muffin!"

And they give him a
BIG BEAR HUG.

SHETLAND LIBRARY